Lighting Our World
A Year of Celebrations

Written by **Catherine Rondina**

Illustrated by **Jacqui Oakley**

KIDS CAN PRESS

For George — the light in my life — C.R.

To Olivia and all your future adventures, to Jamie for your constant support and enthusiasm, and to my parents, who took me on many wondrous childhood trips — J.O.

Acknowledgments

A special thanks to my editors Sheila Barry and Lisa Tedesco for their constant support, Julia Naimska for her wonderful design concepts and Jacqui Oakley, whose beautiful illustrations brought the celebrations to life!

I am grateful for the guidance of the following people and organizations who lent their expertise reviewing the fine details of the celebrations in this book.

Rabbi Jarrod Grover; Diane Taylor Moreau; Suzy Tunzi, Grade 2/3 Teacher at Epiphany of Our Lord Catholic Academy; Rick Monture, Assistant Professor, Indigenous Studies, McMaster University; Angela Chan, Chinese Cultural Centre of Greater Toronto; Chandra Vignarajah, Richmond Hill Hindu Temple; Dr. Mohamed Elhalwagy, President, The Nile Association of Ontario; Kaveh Kalantari, Iranian Association, United Kingdom; Dr. Retta Alemayehu, Ethiopian Association in the Greater Toronto Area and Surrounding Regions; Vietnamese Association, Toronto; Consulate of Sweden, Toronto; Consulate General of the Federal Republic of Germany; Société Saint-Jean-Baptiste de Montréal; Japan Information Centre, Consulate General of Japan; Consulate General of Peru; As-Sadiq Islamic School; Staff of the Toronto Public Library, York Woods District Branch; New Zealand Ministry of Foreign Affairs and Trade.

Photo references of the stove and paddle for the Iroquois Midwinter Ceremony, p. 7, provided courtesy of the Woodland Cultural Centre.

Kids Can Press acknowledges the financial support of the Government of Ontario, through the Ontario Media Development Corporation's Ontario Book Initiative; the Ontario Arts Council; the Canada Council for the Arts; and the Government of Canada, through the BPIDP, for our publishing activity.

Published in Canada by
Kids Can Press Ltd.
25 Dockside Drive
Toronto, ON M5A 0B5

Published in the U.S. by
Kids Can Press Ltd.
2250 Military Road
Tonawanda, NY 14150

www.kidscanpress.com

The artwork in this book was rendered in acrylic paint and ink with some digital touches.
The text is set in Adobe Jenson Pro and Snoopy Snails.

Edited by Sheila Barry and Lisa Tedesco
Designed by Julia Naimska

This book is smyth sewn casebound.
Manufactured in Singapore, in 3/2012 by Tien Wah Press (Pte) Ltd.

CM 12 0 9 8 7 6 5 4 3 2 1

Library and Archives Canada Cataloguing in Publication

Rondina, Catherine
     Lighting our world : a year of celebrations / Catherine Rondina ; illustrated by Jacqui Oakley.

ISBN 978-1-55453-594-1

     1. Festivals — Juvenile literature. 2. Light — Religious aspects — Juvenile literature. 3. Candles and lights — Juvenile literature. I. Oakley, Jacqui II. Title.

GT3933.R66 2012   j394.26   C2011-908683-2

Kids Can Press is a *corus*™ Entertainment company

CONTENTS

Introduction

From busy city streets to small town communities, from familiar neighborhoods to ancient faraway places, people all over the world gather together and use light to celebrate special occasions. Every culture has its own unique set of customs and traditions for celebrating with light. Some use light to welcome the changing seasons, others salute a historic day, some have a spiritual connection, while others honor the dead or celebrate new beginnings. These festivals of light give the world a special glow each and every day of the year. Whether it's the brightness of the sun, the glow of the moon, the flickering of a candle, a lit-up tree or a bonfire, light connects us, warms our hearts and brings us hope for a brighter tomorrow.

Celebrate and shine your light!

Calendars Throughout History

For thousands of years people have wanted to be able to keep track of important events and the passage of time. Just as a clock helps us count the seconds, minutes and hours in a day, a calendar measures time by days, weeks and months.

All calendars are created by following how the sun or the moon (or sometimes both) appear in the sky at different times of the year. The lunar calendar measures time based on the cycles of the moon, which are the different phases or shapes that the moon appears in the sky as it moves around the earth. The Islamic, or Muslim, calendar is an example of a lunar calendar. The solar calendar measures time based on the position of the sun in the sky — how we see the sun as the earth revolves around it. The Gregorian calendar, which is used by most of the world today, is a solar calendar. It divides the solar year into twelve months using the time it takes the earth to travel around the sun — 365.242199 days! Some calendars, called lunisolar calendars, use both the moon's orbit and the earth's orbit. The Chinese calendar and the Jewish, or Hebrew, calendar are both examples of lunisolar calendars. Today, many cultures might regularly use the Gregorian calendar but follow a different calendar to track special religious events.

Ask an adult whether you use the Gregorian calendar or a different one to keep track of your culture's special days. Then create your own calendar for the next twelve months and use it to record any special dates and events that you want to remember.

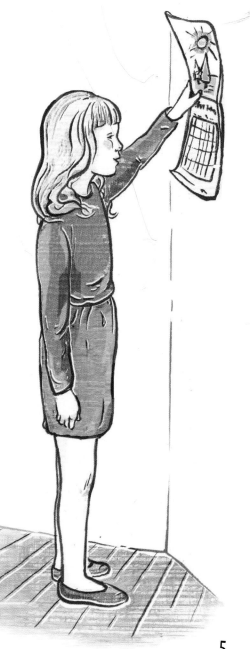

Up Helly Aa
(Shetland Islands, Scotland)

Hello, my name is Sophie. I live with my family in the Shetland Islands in Scotland. On the last Tuesday of January we celebrate *Up Helly Aa*, the largest fire festival in Europe. It's a fun way to remember what life was like in the days of the **Vikings**, who lived here more than one thousand years ago. For many months we work together to build the Galley, a wooden Viking ship, for the celebration. On the day of the big event we dress up in costumes like the Vikings used to wear. Early in the evening we have a Junior Torchlit Procession that's just for kids. As night falls, the Guizer Jarl (say: *gaiser yarl*), our Viking leader, begins the main parade. The men march through town with over one thousand lit torches that they throw into the Galley. Together we watch the red glow of the burning ship as we sing and dance.

Iroquois Midwinter Ceremony (Canada)

In January, five nights after the new moon appears, the people of the **Six Nations** in southern Ontario gather for the Iroquois Midwinter Ceremony. This eight-day ceremony marks the beginning of the new year. During the first two days of the ceremony a custom called "stirring ashes" is performed in a **longhouse**. Two stoves at each end of the longhouse are filled with wooden logs. Once the logs have burned everyone gets a turn to stir the ashes with a special wooden paddle as they give thanks for their blessings and pray for the renewal of the earth.

Chinese New Year (China)

My name is Jian (say: *jyen*), and I live in China. My favorite celebration is Chinese New Year, when we honor our ancestors and the ancient gods. The fun begins on the first day of the first moon and can last the whole month. During this time we have family reunions, buy new clothes and clean our homes to get rid of bad luck. For me, the best part is eating delicious dumplings and getting special red envelopes with money inside. At the end of the celebration we have a beautiful lantern festival, which also includes a parade with a giant paper dragon. This tradition is more than two thousand years old. Red lanterns are lit and hung everywhere for good luck. Fireworks explode in the night, making loud noises that scare evil spirits away.

Sapporo Snow Festival (Japan)

Every February millions of people visit Sapporo, Japan, to enjoy the Snow Festival. This seven-day event, which began in 1950 with some high school students building statues in Odori Park, has become a world-famous contest to see who can build the best snow sculpture. Hundreds of snow statues and ice sculptures can be found on display in Odori Park, the Tsudome (say: *soo-dome-eh*) Site and on the main street in Susukino (say: *soo-soo-key-no*). Some of the sculptures are very small, and others are as big as buildings. At night all the sculptures are lit up with colored lights, candles and spotlights.

Las Fallas (Valencia, Spain)

My name is Belinda, and I live in Valencia, Spain. On the first Sunday of March my city honors Saint Joseph, the **patron saint** of carpenters, with a festival called *Las Fallas*. Our spring celebration keeps builders very busy. *Las Fallas* is like a giant puppet show, and neighborhoods spend months building their own *ninots*, or puppets. The *ninots* are made of papier mâché, wire and wood and are built as large as 15 m (50 ft.). That's as big as five classrooms stacked on top of each other! For five days people visit from around the world to see these incredible puppets. At midnight on the last night of the festival all the *ninots* are burned except for the one voted most popular. It is placed in a special museum. As the *ninots* burn, fireworks light the evening sky. We call it, *Nit del Foc*, Night of Fire, because it looks like the city is on fire!

Carnival (Martinique, Caribbean)

During Lent the people who live on the island of Martinique give up special foods and treats in order to prepare for the **resurrection** of Jesus Christ, which they honor on **Easter** Sunday. Before Lent begins, they have one of the longest carnival parties in the world. There are great parades every night until **Ash Wednesday**, the day they call the Death of King Carnival. On this day everyone on the island dresses in black and white for the funeral parade of Vaval, the Carnival King. He's a decorated **mannequin** who is thrown onto a huge fire to mark the end of the celebrations and the beginning of Lent.

Nowruz (Iran)

My name is Arash, and I live in Iran. I want to tell you about *Nowruz* (say: *nou-rooz*), the ancient festival of our new year. *Nowruz* is celebrated in March on the first full day of spring and lasts for thirteen days. On the eve of the last Wednesday of the old year, people celebrate in the streets and make bonfires to jump over. Some believe the fire will burn away all their fears and bring good luck for the new year. We prepare for *Nowruz* by cleaning our houses and buying new clothes. On the first day, my family gathers around the table with the Haft Seen, seven special objects that bring us a good new year. During the next few days relatives and friends come to visit and we eat lots of pastries and dried fruits. The last day of the celebration is spent outdoors with family and friends having fun!

Holi (India)

In India, Hindus celebrate *Holi*, a festival that welcomes spring and honors the **Hindu** legend of good overcoming evil. On the first day people clean their houses and collect old wooden furniture and branches for the evening's bonfires. A mannequin of Holika representing the evil aunt who tried to harm her good nephew Prahlad to punish him for his beliefs is also put on the fire. Based on the Hindu legend, she carries him into the fire but he survives and she dies. The next day is the Festival of Colors, a day of fun for all ages. On this day of celebration people wear old clothes and go out into the streets and throw colored powder at each other.

Walpurgis Night (Sweden)

My name is Anna, and I live in Sweden. Every April 30 we celebrate *Walpurgis* (say: *vahl-poor-gis*) Night, a festival welcoming spring. On this night bonfires are lit with old wood that people have been gathering for months. This tradition originated in Germany, and the custom came to Sweden during the eighteenth century. Bonfires were lit to scare away predators from cattle, and some even believed the fires would frighten away evil spirits. Today this festival is enjoyed by university students, who light huge bonfires and set off firecrackers to celebrate the end of school exams. As the fires burn, people throw in old boxes, wooden doors and dried tree branches as a choir sings. Once the fire burns down, everyone enjoys a warm bowl of soup made from nettles, the first weed to grow once the snow has melted.

Easter (Germany)

In Germany, Easter weekend is one of the most popular **Christian** celebrations of the year. The festivities begin on Good Friday, a day set aside for people to fast and reflect on the sacrifices their Lord, Jesus Christ, made for them. On Holy Saturday some families spend the evening at church. That same night a big Easter fire is built in the middle of town where branches and twigs are thrown onto the fire. It's like saying good-bye to winter and hello to spring. Easter Sunday is a special time for children. Parents hide chocolate bunnies, hand-painted Easter eggs and small gifts for children to find.

Cinco de Mayo (United States)

Hi, my name is Miguel. I live in Los Angeles, California, in the United States. My grandparents immigrated here from Mexico. We are Americans now, but we are still very proud of our Mexican heritage. That is why we have so much fun celebrating *Cinco de Mayo* (say: *cin-co de may-yo*), which means the Fifth of May. On this day in 1862 the Mexican army defeated France in the battle of Puebla. In honor of this day we celebrate with Mexican food and mariachi music, and everywhere you look there is red, white and green — the colors of the Mexican flag. At night people decorate their backyards with tiny white lights that twinkle, as the skies light up with fireworks!

Buddha's Birthday (South Korea)

During the month of May, many South Koreans celebrate **Buddha's** birthday. Buddhists follow their calendar based on the phases of the moon, so the date of Buddha's birthday changes every year. As part of the celebrations **temples** and streets are decorated with fresh lotus flowers and paper lanterns, which come in many different colors. Inside the temples people burn **incense**, light candles and pray for Buddha's blessings. At night, in the capital city of Seoul, hundreds of people take part in the Lantern Festival and parade through the streets for miles and miles with their lanterns lit in honor of Buddha.

Inti Raymi (Cusco, Peru)

Hello, my name is Valentina, and I live in Cusco, Peru. Every June 24 thousands of people come here to visit Sacsayhuamán (say: *sac-say-wa-man*). It is an **Incan** stone ruin where actors dress in traditional clothing and re-enact an ancient ceremony called *Inti Raymi*, or Festival of the Sun. The Incas believed that the Sun was a very important ruler. During the ceremony the Sapa Inca, the Emperor, takes center stage and prays to the sun. Throughout the ceremony actors dance and sing in celebration. As the sun sets, big stacks of straw are set on fire to welcome the new cycle of life. As part of the performance, actors pretend to sacrifice a llama to ensure that the crops will be plentiful for the next year. The Sapa Inca then offers a blessing to the people and a new year begins.

Saint-Jean-Baptiste Day (Canada)

For French Canadians across Canada, June 24 is Saint-Jean-Baptiste Day, a time to express great cultural pride. Celebrations take place from coast to coast with fun-filled parades, street parties and fireworks that fill the early summer skies with color. This special day once combined the ancient traditions of the **summer solstice**, including symbols of light such as bonfires, with honoring the patron saint of French Canadians, Saint-Jean-Baptiste. Today the festivities are about celebrating the great pride of French Canadians!

19

Let's Celebrate!

Almost every country in the world has a day to celebrate its founding or independence. It's like a birthday party for the nation. Many celebrations include music, speeches, parties and of course lots of colorful fireworks. Here are a few countries that celebrate in the month of July.

Canada

Hello! I'm Nathan.
On July 1 Canadians celebrate the day Canada became a country, also known as Canada Day. There is music, parades with the Royal Canadian Mounted Police, and the red-and-white maple leaf flag is everywhere!

United States

Hi! I'm Madison.
On July 4 Americans across the United States celebrate Independence Day. There are picnics and parades, and everywhere you look you see red, white and blue flags waving in the wind.

Argentina

Hola (say: *oh-la*)! I'm Ricardo.
On July 9, Argentina celebrates its independence. A flag hangs outside of almost every house. We have big outdoor festivals and the sound of honking car horns can be heard everywhere.

France

Bonjour! I'm Zoe.
Every July 14 over one million people come to Paris to celebrate Bastille Day. On this day in 1789 the French fought for their rights over the king and queen. In celebration of this event, the Bastille monument is decorated with French flags and the Eiffel Tower is lit up.

Belgium

Hallo (say: *hah-low*)!
I'm Thomas.
July 21 is our national day, and Belgians come to celebrate in the capital city of Brussels. The streets are filled with musicians, live plays and parades. Everyone wears black, yellow and red and joins in the fun.

Bahamas

Hi! I'm Alesha.
I live in the Bahamas. Our islands celebrate independence in July and it's a weeklong party. The biggest celebration takes place on July 10. That's when the parades and festivals have everyone dancing in the streets!

Obon (Japan)

My name is Kiyoto (say: *kee-yoh-toh*) and I live in Japan. In August my family celebrates *Obon* (say: *OH-bone*), the Buddhist Festival of the Dead. Buddhists believe that during this time the souls of the dead come home to be with their families. In preparation, we clean our houses and decorate *butsudans* (say: *but-su-dan*), small Buddhist altars, with fruits, vegetables and sweets to welcome them. We build small bonfires, called welcoming flames, in front of our houses to guide the spirits back home. The best part of the festival is *Obon Odori*, when we dance to traditional Japanese music in neighborhood parks wearing **kimonos**. On the final evening of the festival we say good-bye to our ancestors' spirits with a ceremony called *Tōrō Nagashi*. We light lanterns and place them in the river and watch as they float away.

Chung Yuan (China)

In China, August is known as Ghost Month. During *Chung Yuan* (say: *y-ew-ae-n*) some people don't like to go out after dark for fear that ghosts will come to haunt them. To make the spirits happy the Chinese have a party midway through the month. During this party water lanterns are lit and released into the sea. It is believed that good fortune will come to the family whose lantern floats away the fastest. Many streets and graveyards are filled with paper models of gifts to the ghosts, including paper money. At night, the paper gifts are all burned in huge piles in honor of the spooky guests.

TeT Trung Thu (VieTnam)

My name is Ly (say: *lee*), and in my country, Vietnam, we have a children's festival called *Tet Trung Thu* (say: *tet-troony-too*). It is a very popular family holiday, when parents spend time with their children after the busy harvest season. During the festival, my sisters and I sing and dance in a street parade. We perform traditional Vietnamese songs and carry colorful lanterns that are lit and shaped like fish and stars. My favorite is the spinning lantern that has a lit candle inside of it. It moves just like the earth circling the sun. For a treat we eat *Banh Trung Thu* (say: *bawn-troony-too*), or moon cakes. They are filled with lotus seeds, ground beans and orange peels and have a bright center that looks just like the moon!

Enkutatash (Ethiopia)

On September 11 the people of Ethiopia celebrate their new year. The festival is called *Enkutatash* (say: *inqu-ta-ta-sh*), meaning Gift of Jewels. It dates back to when the queen of Sheba returned from a visit with King Solomon of Jerusalem and her chiefs welcomed her with jewels. This spring festival also marks the end of the season of the long rains, a time when the Ethiopian Highlands are covered in wild flowers. As part of the celebration girls dress in new clothes, sing and dance through the villages and hand out flowers to everyone. At night, every home lights a bonfire, and boys sing and dance throughout the villages as fireworks light the sky.

Diwali (India)

Hi! My name is Sanjay, and I live in India. Like other Hindus (say: *HIN-doo*), my family celebrates *Diwali* (say: *dee-WAHL-ee*), which means Row of Lights. Hindus follow the lunar calendar, so *Diwali* is celebrated for five days in October or November. This festival honors Lakshmi (say: *LUCK-shmee*), the goddess of wealth, luck and happiness. We use special decorations to invite Lakshmi into our homes. My friends and I paint *rangolis*, patterns made of colored paste mixed with water, outside on the walls and floors of our homes. We also light *diyas* (say: *dee-yah*), small candles, and place them in our windows and around our shops and temples. Hindus believe that Lakshmi will visit the houses with the brightest lights. A visit from her means good luck for the whole year!

Halloween

On October 31, children from Canada, the United States, the United Kingdom and Ireland love to celebrate Halloween. This celebration dates back to the ancient **Celtics**, who believed the dead roamed the earth on this spooky night. They would carve frightening faces into turnips or potatoes, light them with a candle and place them outside their homes to scare evil spirits away. Today, people carve pumpkins or jack-o'-lanterns with scary or silly faces and light them with candles just for fun. Kids also dress up in costumes, knock on their neighbors' doors and yell "trick or treat" with hopes of getting candy.

Ramadan (Egypt)

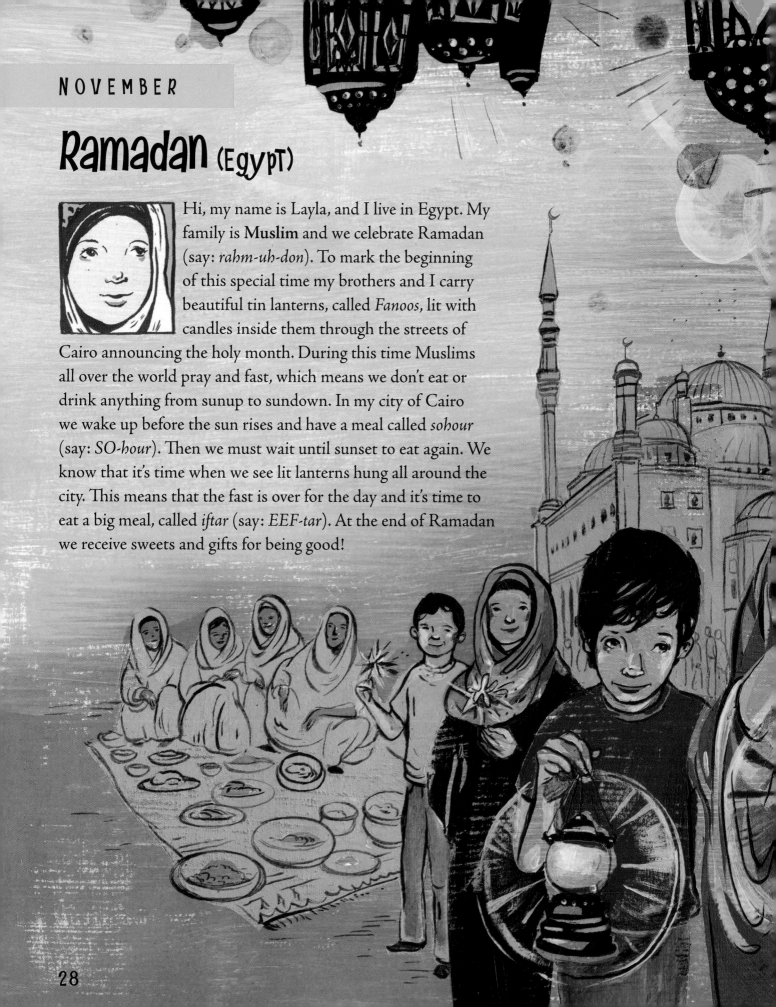

Hi, my name is Layla, and I live in Egypt. My family is **Muslim** and we celebrate Ramadan (say: *rahm-uh-don*). To mark the beginning of this special time my brothers and I carry beautiful tin lanterns, called *Fanoos*, lit with candles inside them through the streets of Cairo announcing the holy month. During this time Muslims all over the world pray and fast, which means we don't eat or drink anything from sunup to sundown. In my city of Cairo we wake up before the sun rises and have a meal called *sohour* (say: *SO-hour*). Then we must wait until sunset to eat again. We know that it's time when we see lit lanterns hung all around the city. This means that the fast is over for the day and it's time to eat a big meal, called *iftar* (say: *EEF-tar*). At the end of Ramadan we receive sweets and gifts for being good!

Guy Fawkes Day (New Zealand)

In New Zealand, which was once part of the British Empire, people still follow traditional celebrations, such as Guy Fawkes Day, which is celebrated on November 5. On this night in 1605 Guy Fawkes tried to blow up the king of England and the parliament with barrels of gunpowder. Luckily his plan didn't work and he was caught. In remembrance of this day, the people of New Zealand celebrate how fortunate the government was to have escaped by lighting the night sky with fireworks, bonfires and sparklers.

Hanukkah (Israel)

Hi! My name is Ari, and I live in Israel. This time of year I share a special celebration along with other Jewish people called Hanukkah (say: *HAH-nu-kah*), or the Festival of Lights. Each night, for eight nights, we light one of the candles on the *menorah*. The candles help us remember a miracle that took place more than two thousand years ago when a group of brave Jewish men, called the Maccabees, fought off the Greeks and saved their temple. After the victory they went to light an oil lamp and found it had enough oil for only one night. But to everyone's amazement the oil burned for eight nights! During our celebration, my brothers and sisters and I receive small gifts and we play the *dreidel* game.

Christmas (England)

In England, as in other places around the world, Christians celebrate the birth of Jesus Christ on December 25. For many the celebrations begin weeks before by decorating homes and storefronts with lots of colorful lights. Many people also put up an evergreen tree in their home and cover it with lights and decorations. A shining star is often placed at the top of the tree to remember the star in the sky that the Three Wise Men followed to Bethlehem to visit Jesus.

On December 24, Christmas Eve, the fun begins with children and adults singing Christmas carols. On Christmas Day, many families attend church services and then gather together with friends for a Christmas feast of roast turkey and plum pudding. As part of the holiday tradition, many people also listen to the queen's yearly Christmas message. But before that, they open up gifts that Father Christmas (also known as Santa Claus) leaves under the Christmas tree!

Kwanzaa (United States)

From December 26 to January 1, African-Americans celebrate the seven days of *Kwanzaa* (say: *kwan-zaa*). It is a festival to celebrate the history of their African ancestors. Every night of the celebration children light one of the seven candles of the *kinara* (say: *kee-nah-rah*), a special candleholder. The seven candles, one black, three green and three red, represent each of the seven principles of *Kwanzaa*. During the celebration everyone sips from the unity cup, a symbol of unity among the African nations. They also eat meals much like their African ancestors did and decorate their houses in red, black and green, the colors that symbolize Africa.

Glossary

Ash Wednesday: the first day of Lent, when Christians go to church and have ashes placed on their foreheads in remembrance of the death of Jesus Christ

Buddha: the Indian religious leader and teacher who founded the religion Buddhism

Celtics: a group of Indo-European peoples, such as the Irish, Scottish and Welsh

Christian: someone who follows the religion and teachings of Jesus Christ

Dreidel: a four-sided spinning top with a letter from the Hebrew alphabet on each side

Easter: a yearly Christian festival and holiday celebrated on the first Sunday after the first full moon on or after March 21. On this day Christians remember when Jesus came back from the dead.

Hinduism: a religion and philosophy practiced mainly in India. Hindus worship one god who takes many forms.

Inca: a member of the Aboriginal peoples who ruled Peru before being defeated by Spain in the sixteenth century

Incense: a substance that is burned to produce a pleasant smell

Jesus: worshiped by Christians as the son of God

Kimono: a long, loose Japanese robe that is held in place with a sash

Lent: forty days from Ash Wednesday to Easter, when Christians fast and pray

Longhouse: a large rectangular one-room wooden frame structure used by the people of the Six Nations for special cultural ceremonies

Mannequin: a life-sized form of a human body used to display clothing, also known as a dummy

Menorah: a candleholder for nine candles used during Hanukkah

Muslim: someone who follows the religion of Islam

Patron saint: a saint regarded as the special guardian of a certain occupation, place or group of people

Resurrection: to return to life

Six Nations: a group of Iroquois peoples that includes the Mohawk, Oneida, Onondaga, Cayuga, Seneca and Tuscarora

Summer Solstice: happens on June 21. It is the longest day in the northern hemisphere, when the sun is at its most northern point in the sky.

Temple: a building people attend to worship and pray

Vikings: Scandinavian sea warriors and traders who raided many countries between the eighth and eleventh centuries